ANIMAL STRIKE
AT THE ZOO

BY **KARMA WILSON**

ILLUSTRATED BY

MARGARET SPENGLER

HarperCollins Publishers

Library of Congress Cataloging-in-Publication Data
Wilson, Karma.   Animal strike at the zoo. It's true! / by Karma Wilson ;
illustrated by Margaret Spengler.— 1st ed.   p.   cm.
Summary: The zoo animals go on strike until the tears of a disappointed
little girl make them realize that they actually like what they do.
ISBN-10: 0-06-057502-6 (trade bdg.) — ISBN-13: 978-0-06-057502-1 (trade bdg.)
ISBN-10: 0-06-057503-4 (lib. bdg.) — ISBN-13: 978-0-06-057503-8 (lib. bdg.)
[1. Zoo animals—Fiction. 2. Zoos—Fiction. 3. Strikes and lockouts—Fiction. 4. Stories in rhyme.]
I. Spengler, Margaret, ill. II. Title. PZ8.3.W6976An 2006
[E]—dc22   2005014514
CIP   AC

Typography by Carla Weise
1 2 3 4 5 6 7 8 9 10
❖
First Edition

To Regina, Alan, Chandra, Sabrina, Tyler, and Caleb—
life in your house is as busy as a zoo!
Thank heavens Mommy and Daddy never go on strike.
God bless you all.
—K.W.

To Ken,
my best friend and biggest supporter.
—M.S.

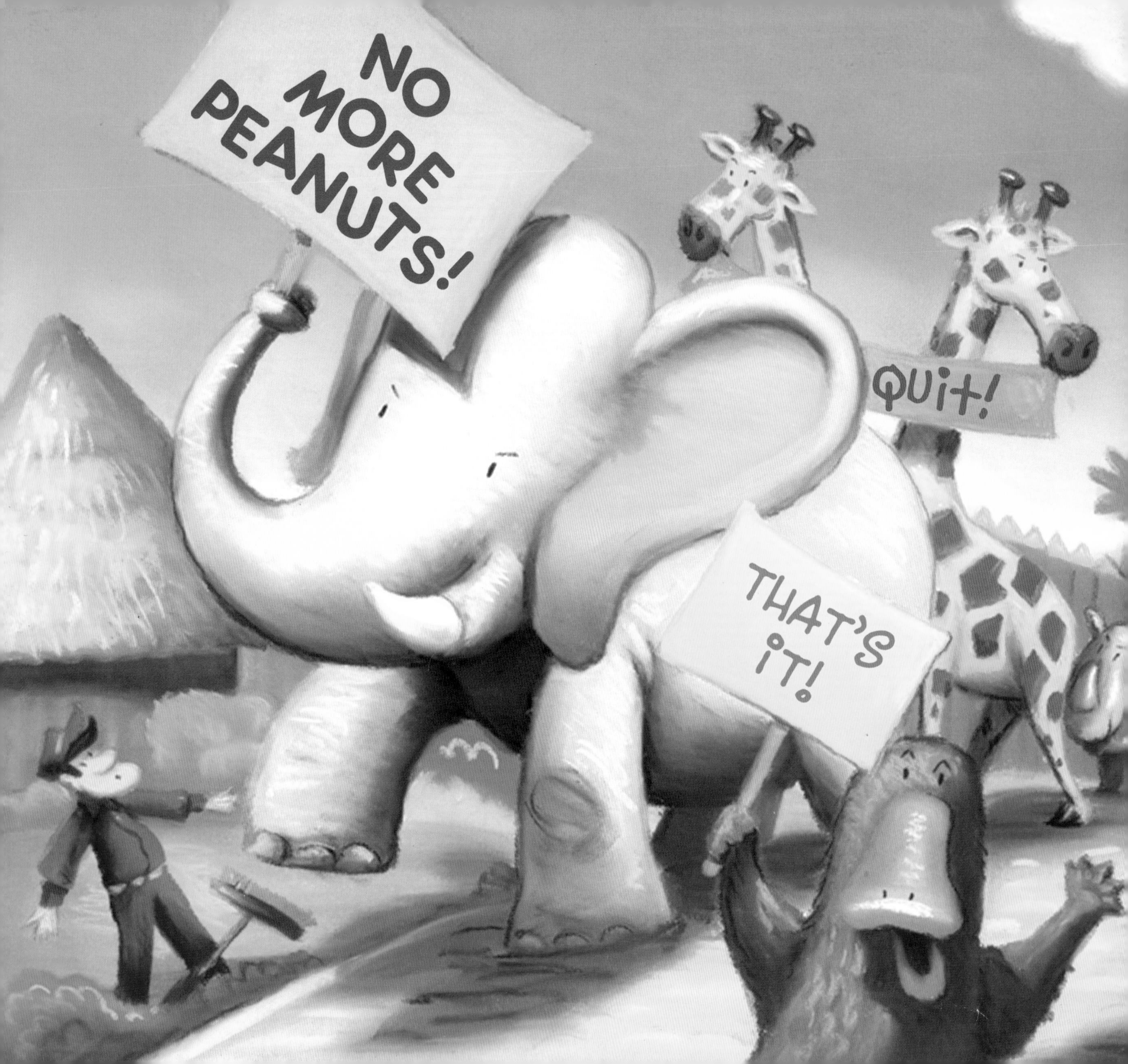
NO MORE PEANUTS!
QUIT!
THAT'S IT!

There's an animal strike at the zoo. It's true!
The headlines are telling it all.
The animals quit. "That's it!" "We're through!"
Say all critters from biggest to small.

"We're paid only peanuts!" the elephants shout.

"And goodness, we're bigger than that."

So now they won't trumpet or lumber about.

They sit in the shade, looking fat.

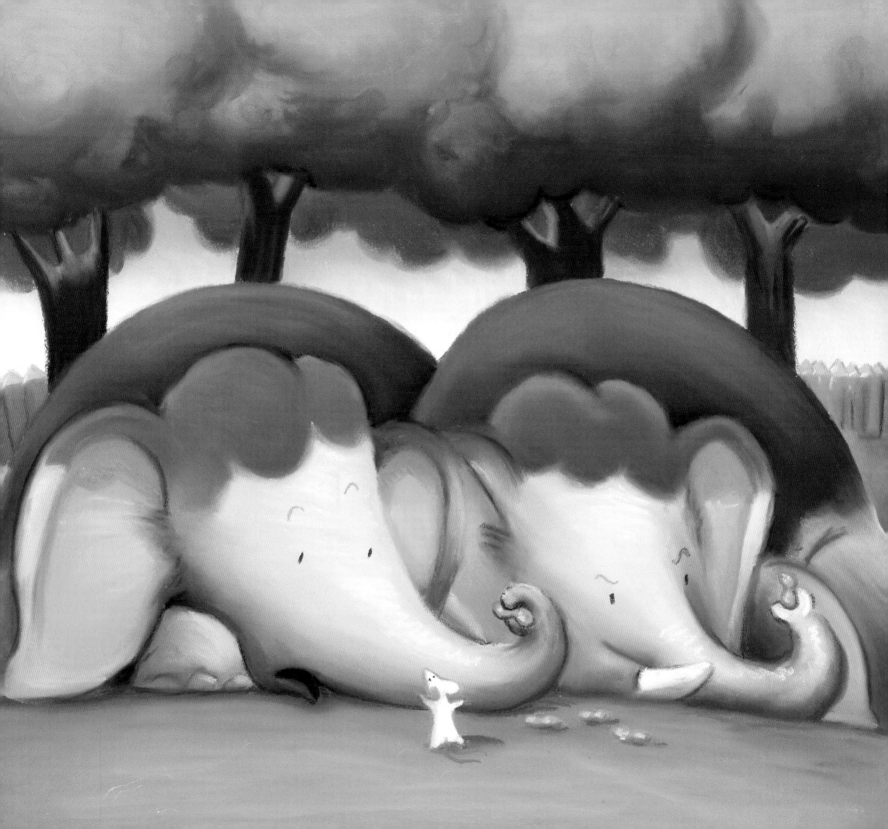

The monkeys won't monkey around anymore.

"You won't see us climbing again!"

They wallow like big monkey lumps on the floor.

"We want a nice pool in our pen!"

The leopards aren't prowling.

The wolf packs aren't howling.

The tigers aren't growling.

The otters are scowling.

EGAD! The worst has come true.
There's an animal strike at the zoo!

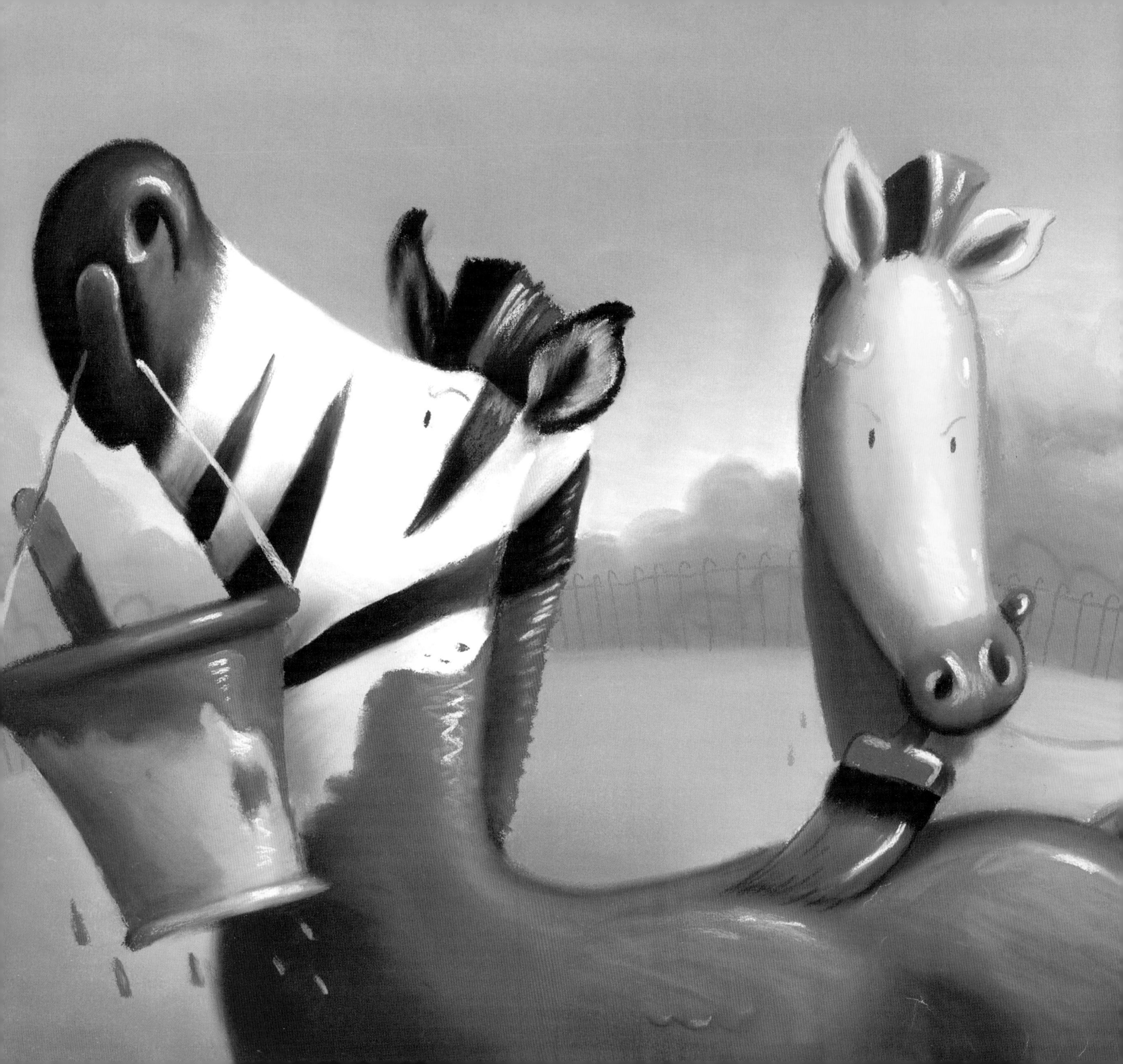

The zebras are looking like horses today.
They painted their stripes in, you see.
"We're all sick and tired of eating this hay!
Our good looks do NOT come for free!"

Those silly giraffes are not any better.

"You won't see our necks anymore!"

They're knitting themselves lots of turtleneck sweaters,

Which go from their heads to the floor!

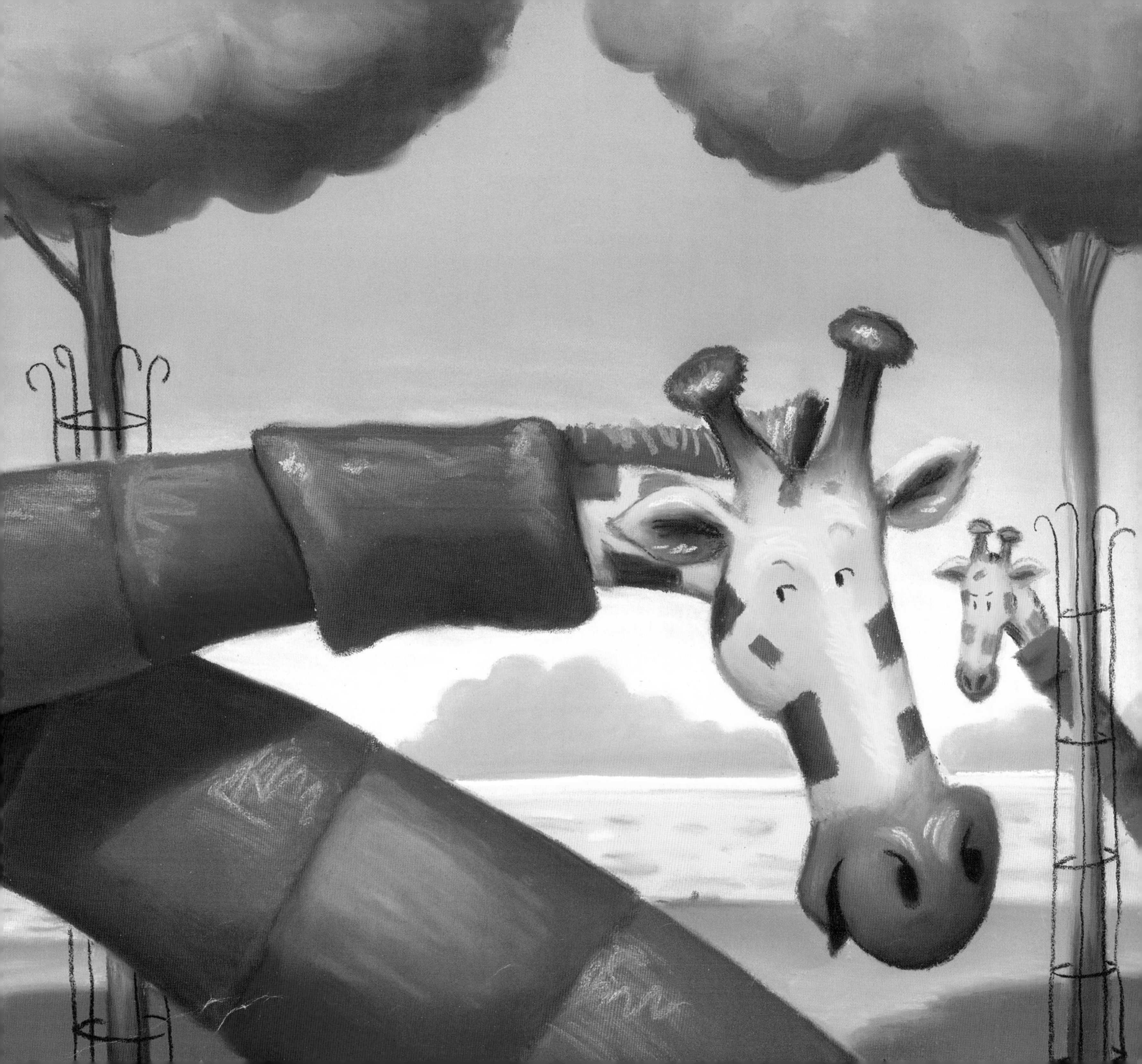

Business these days is as slow as can be.

Folks go to the circus instead.

Nobody wants to pay money to see

The animals lying in bed!

The lions aren't roaring.

The eagles aren't soaring.

The penguins are snoring.

It's all rather boring.

What can the zookeeper do?

There's an animal strike at the zoo!

He really is doing the best that he can.

The elephants all got a raise.

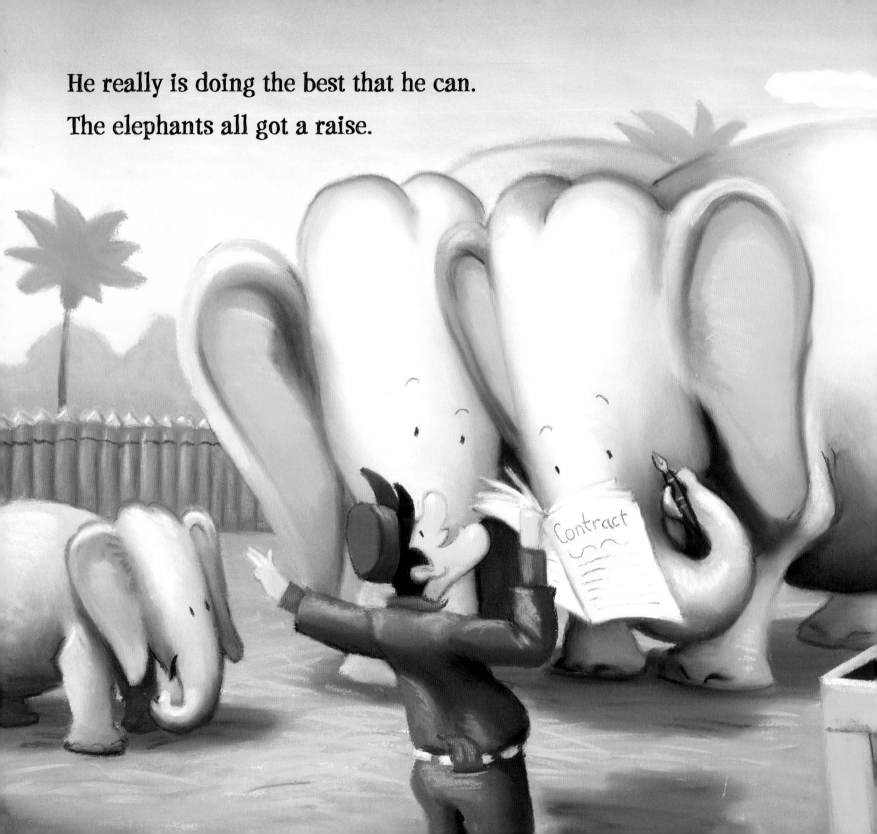

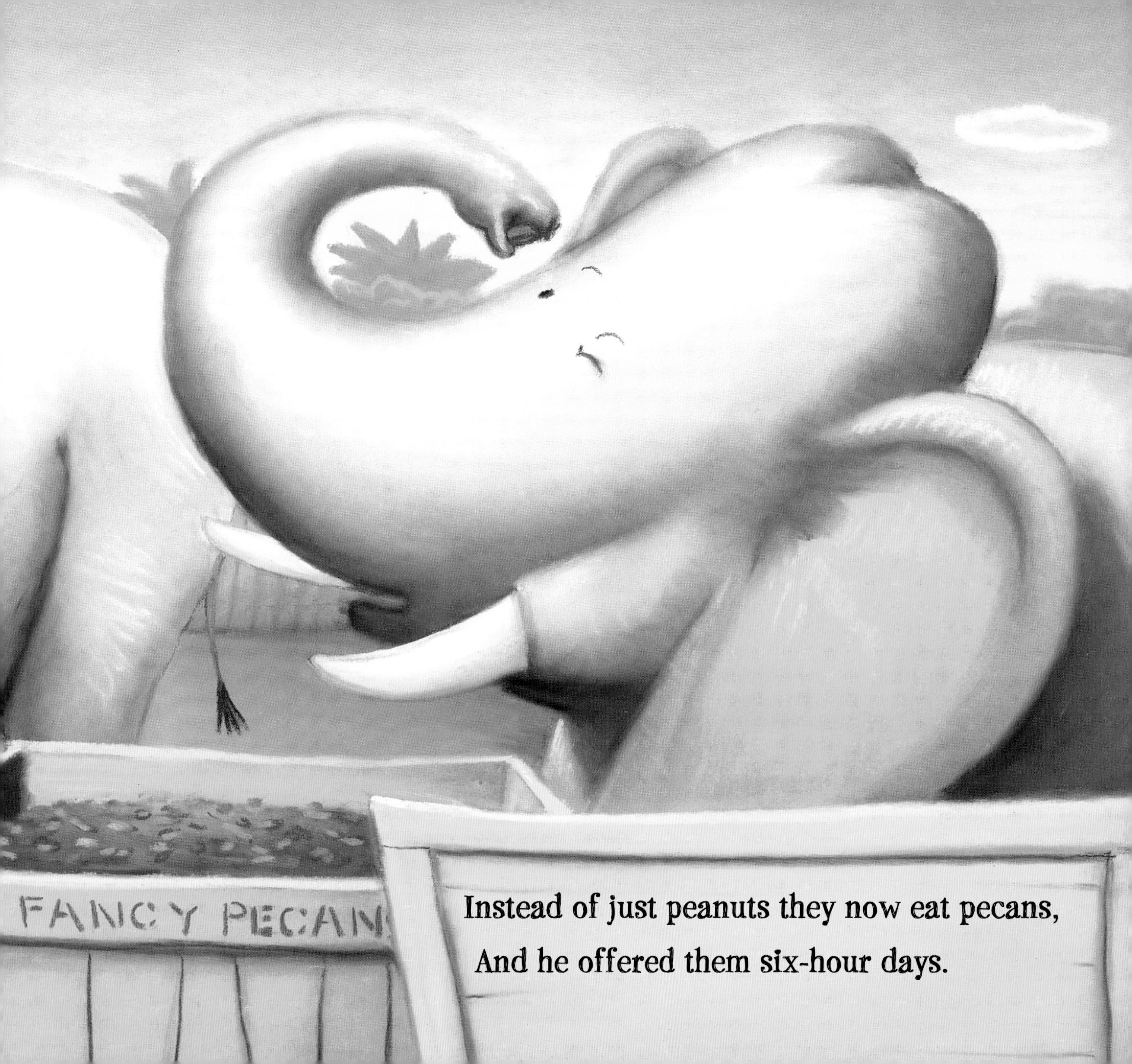
FANCY PECAN

Instead of just peanuts they now eat pecans,
And he offered them six-hour days.

The monkeys were given a small kiddy pool,
And he's feeding the zebras sweet oats.

But the monkeys complain that the water is cool,
And the zebras demand root-beer floats!

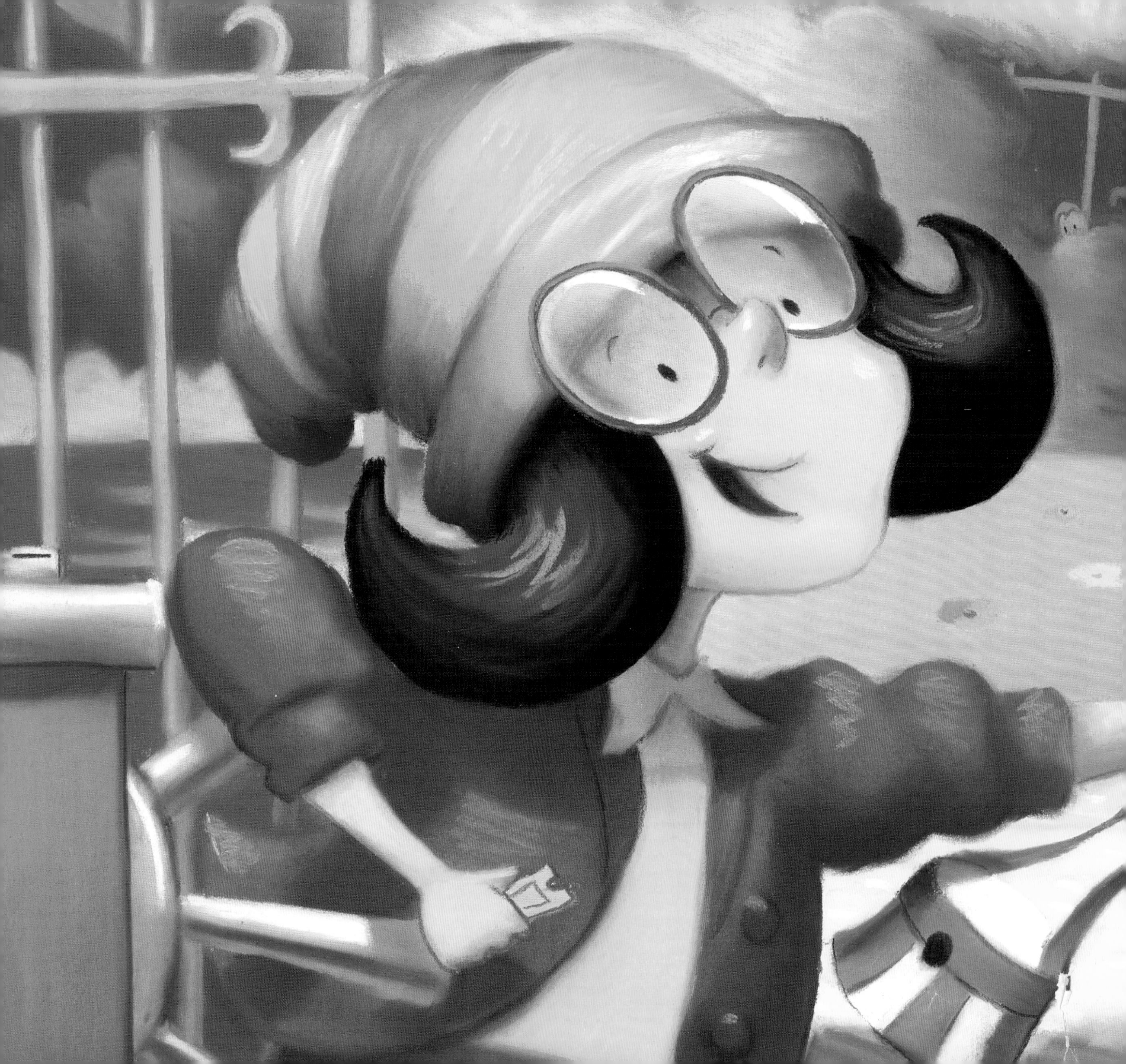

Then in through the gate walks sweet little Sue.

She just can't believe that she's here!

She's always wanted to come to the zoo,

And she's begged for this trip for a year.

But . . .

No birdies are peeping.

No lizards are creeping.

No bunnies are leaping.

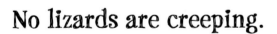

Then poor Sue starts weeping.

Her heart is broken in two . . .

By the animal strike at the zoo!

As tears start to streak down her cute, rosy face,

The animals watch that wee child.

A deep hush of sadness falls over the place . . .

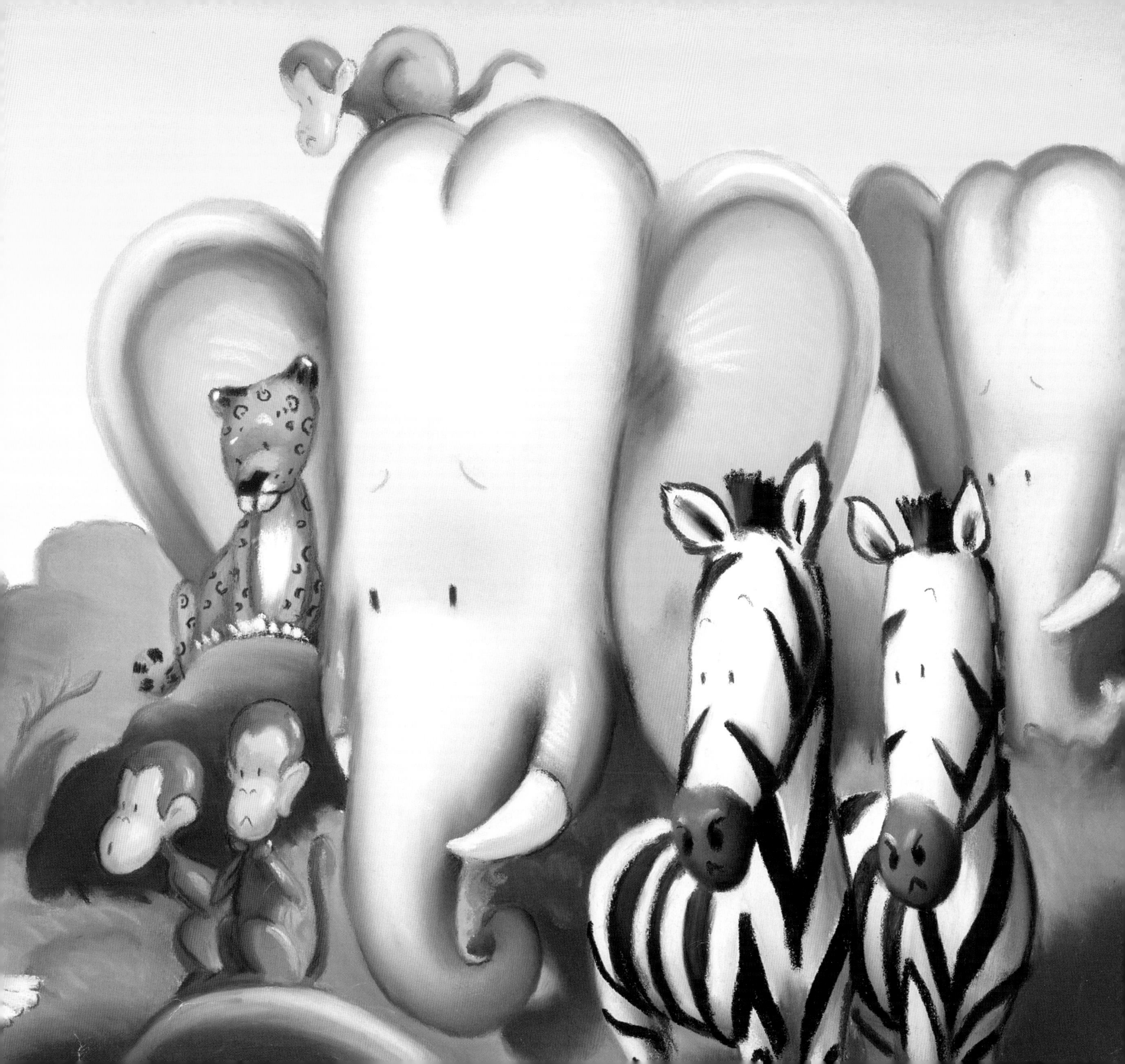

And then they go

TOTALLY WILD!

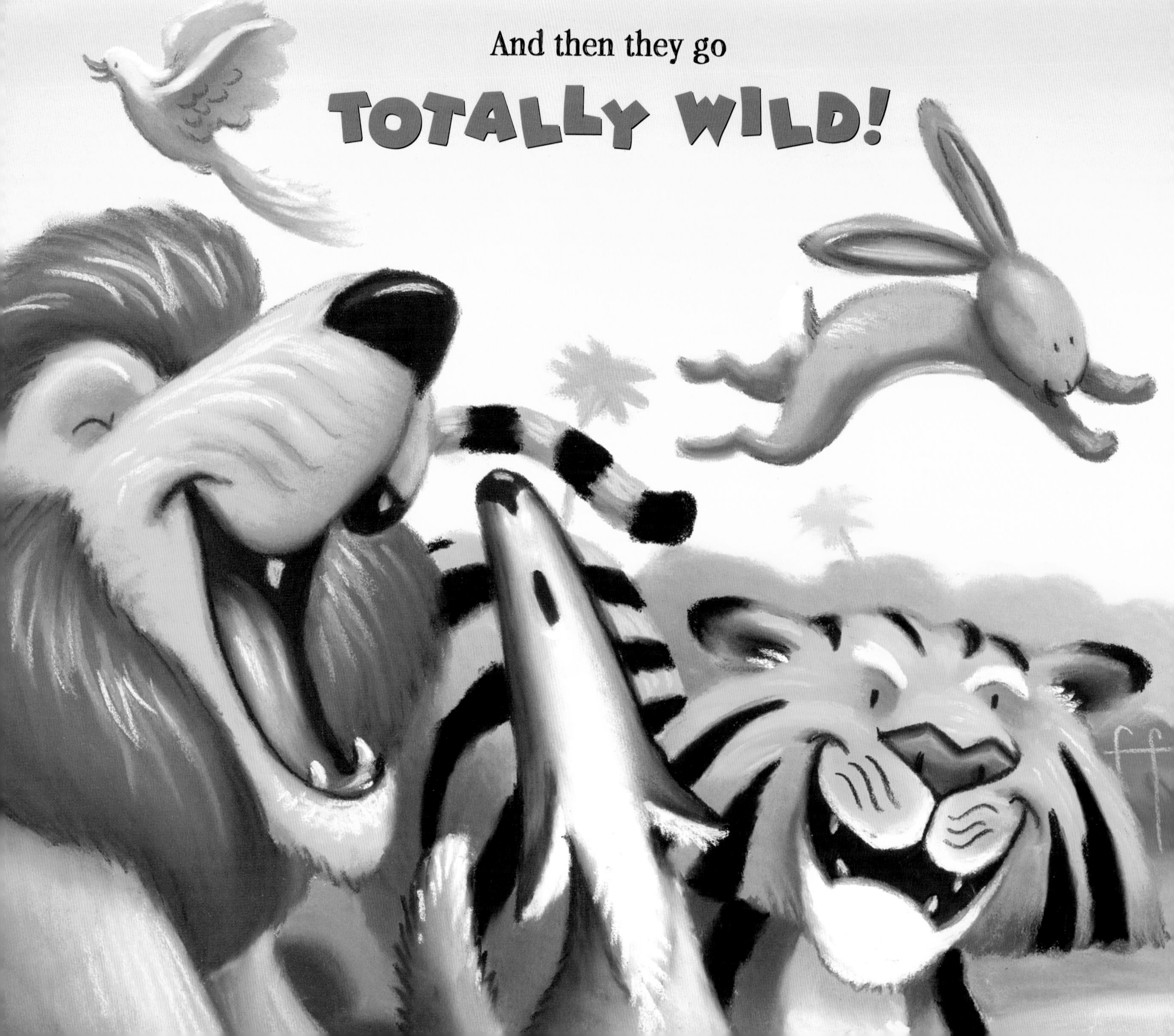

With roaring and peeping and howling and growling,

All critters from biggest to small

Start soaring and creeping and leaping and prowling. . .

Then little Sue laughs at them all!

And all of the animals find out that day
They actually like what they do.
The zookeeper calls the reporters to say,

"HURRAY! NO MORE STRIKE AT THE ZOO!"

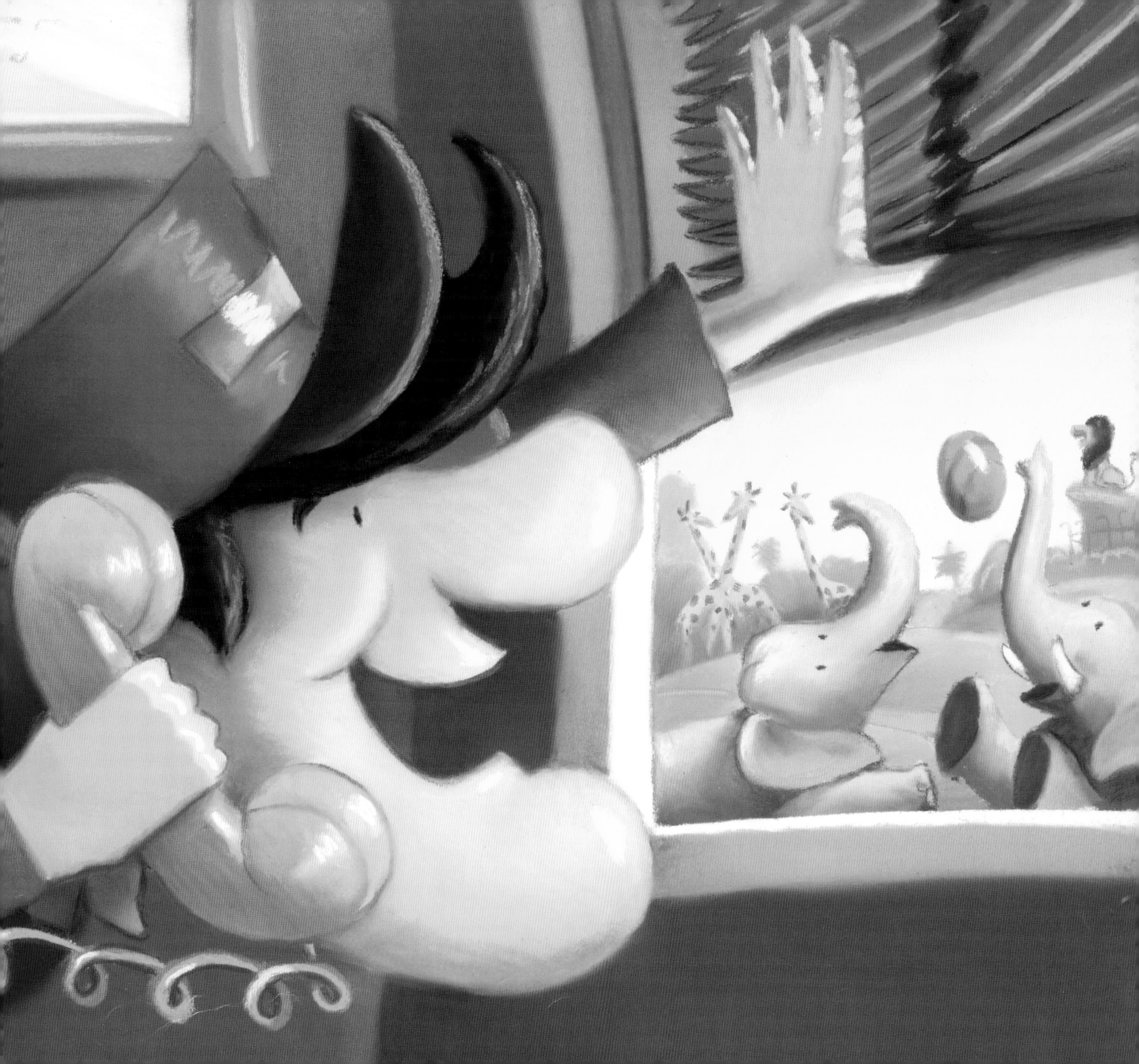

But . . .

The bear at the circus won't pedal his bike.

Uh-oh. He says he's on strike.

Little Red Riding Hood

First published in the UK in 2005 by Mercury Junior
An imprint of Mercury Books
20 Bloomsbury Street, London WC1B 3JH

This book was conceived, edited and designed by
McRae Books Srl
Borgo Santa Croce, 8,
50122 Florence, Italy
info@mcraebooks.com

Project Director: Anne McRae
Design Director: Marco Nardi
Text: Elizabeth McLeod
Illustrations: Maria Mantovani, Renzo Barsotti
Layout & Editing: McRae Books
Cover design: Open Door Ltd

Color separations: R.A.F., Florence
Printed and bound in China

Title: Little Red Riding Hood
ISBN: 1 904668 57 7

Little Red Riding Hood

Illustrators
MARIA MANTOVANI & RENZO BARSOTTI

Mercury
Junior

Once upon a time there was a little girl who was very kind to everyone in her village. One day her grandmother, who loved her granddaughter very much, gave her a red riding cape with a big red hood.

The little girl thought her new cape was wonderful and she put it on straight away. She said she would wear it wherever she went. In such a bright colour, the little girl could be seen from far away, and very soon everyone began calling her Little Red Riding Hood.

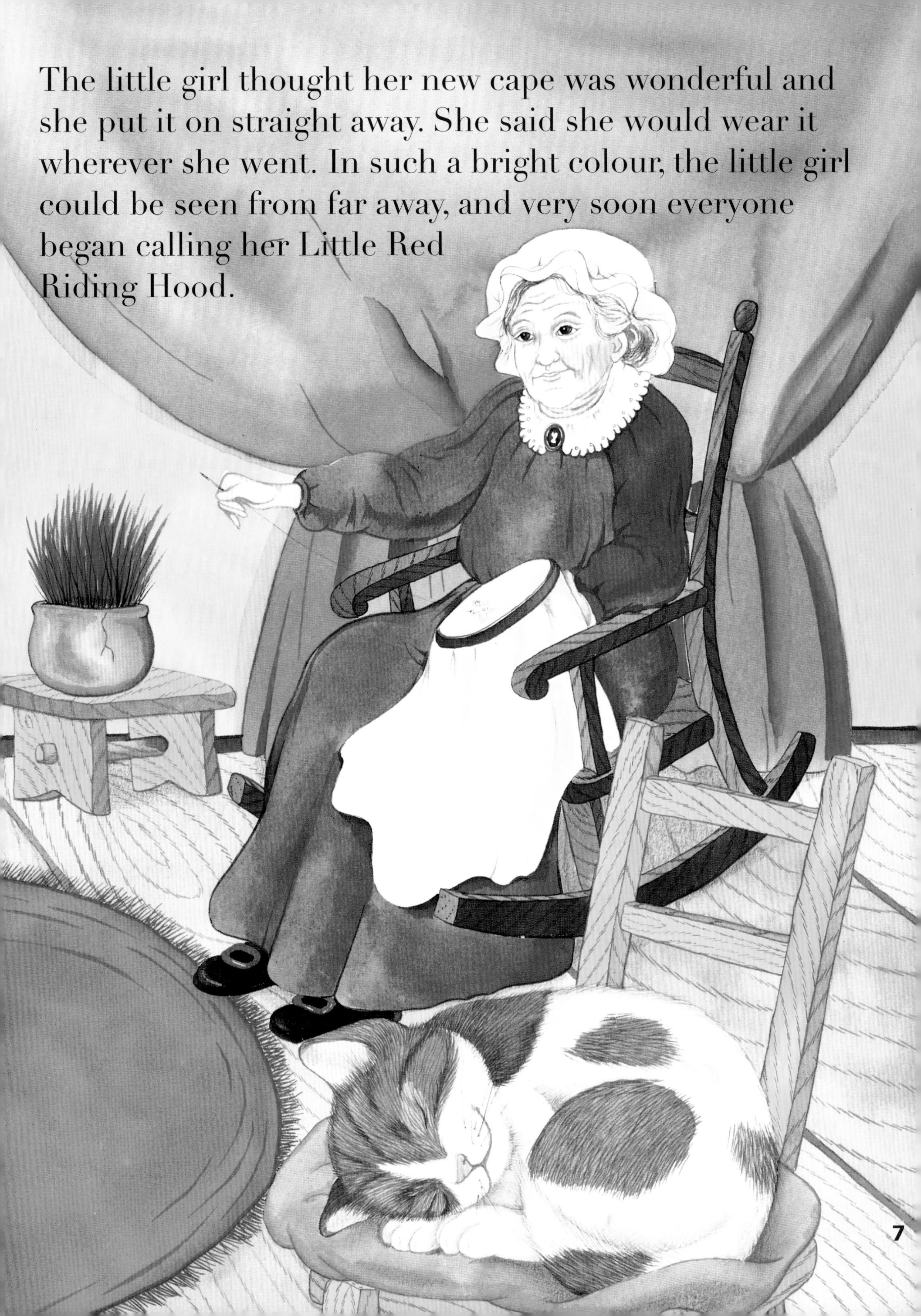

Early one morning, Little Red Riding Hood's mother asked her to visit her grandmother, who was ill and needed medicine and food. She gave her some fresh bread and a bottle of wine to take to her grandmother. "Go straight to your grandmother's house and don't go wandering in the wood," her mother warned.

8

"And when you get there, be polite and say 'Good Day'
to your grandmother, and don't go looking into her
drawers and wardrobe."

9

Little Red Riding Hood's grandmother lived
in a little cottage in the middle of a big wood
quite a long way from the village. It took
about half an hour to get there.

10

So off Little Red Riding
Hood went. She had just entered the wood when she
met a wolf. "Good Day Little Red Riding Hood," said the
Wolf. Since he was such a well mannered and
handsome wolf, Little Red Riding Hood replied
politely, "Good Day Mr Wolf."

"Where are you going all by yourself so early in the morning?" asked the Wolf. "To my grandmother's house. She is ill and I am taking her this fresh bread and bottle of wine to help her get better," she replied.

The Wolf was clever and he was really thinking that this little girl would make a tasty morsel. He did not frighten her, however, because he wanted to eat her grandmother too!

"Tell me, where does your grandmother live?" the Wolf asked. "In a cottage about quarter of an hour's walk from here," said Little Red Riding Hood, who was always very polite.

"What a long way!" said the Wolf,
"why don't you rest a while
and pick a few of these pretty
flowers for your grandmother?"
"That's a good idea!" said
Little Red Riding Hood.

15

Little Red Riding Hood left the main path and began picking flowers. She gathered a large and beautiful bunch for her grandmother.

Then suddenly she remembered her mother's words. "Go straight to your grandmother's house," her mother had said. Little Red Riding Hood went back to the path and started walking to her grandmother's house.

In the meantime, the
Wolf had left Little Red Riding Hood
and had found her grandmother's house.
He knocked quietly on the door.

18

"Who's there?" asked the old lady.
"Little Red Riding Hood, Grandma. I
have fresh bread and good wine from
Mummy to make you feel better," the
Wolf said in a high-pitched voice.
"Open the door and let yourself in.
I'm too sick to get out of bed."

The Wolf slowly opened the cottage door and leapt into the old lady's bedroom. Before the grandmother could call out for help, she had been swallowed up whole by the Wolf.

20

Then the Wolf put on the grandmother's long
nightgown and frilly nightcap, and clambered into
her warm bed. He pulled the covers right up to his
chin and waited.

21

A few minutes later Little Red Riding Hood arrived. She was a little surprised to find the door open. "Good Day Grandma," she called, but there was no reply. She went into the room to see if her grandmother was better or worse.

22

"But Grandma!" she exclaimed, "what big eyes you've got!" "All the better to see you with," came the reply.

"But Grandma! What a big nose you've got!" "All the better to smell you with," came the reply. "But Grandma! What enormous teeth you've got!"

"All the better to eat you with!" growled the Wolf, who suddenly jumped out of bed and swallowed the poor girl whole.

After so much food the Wolf felt very tired, so he climbed back into bed. He soon fell asleep and began to snore. The snoring was so loud that a huntsman, passing by the little cottage, heard the noise and decided to go and see if the old lady was well.

The huntsman went into the cottage and could not believe his eyes. There was a Wolf wearing a nightgown and frilly cap, fast asleep in bed! Suddenly a strange sound came from the Wolf's stomach. The huntsman got out his knife and cut open the Wolf's stomach.

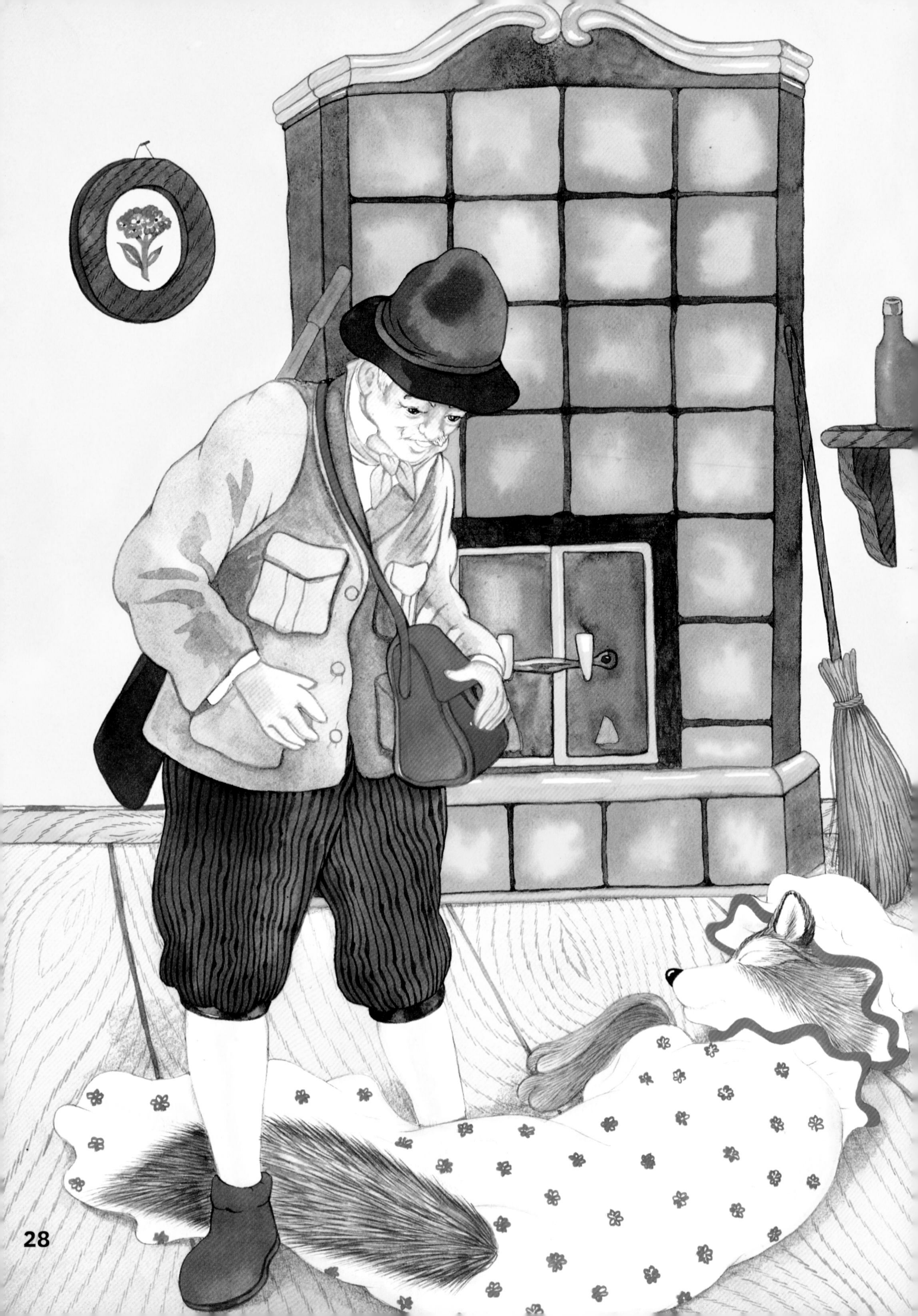

And...surprise! Out of the Wolf's stomach came Little Red Riding Hood and her grandmother. Although shaken by their adventure, they were both happy to be alive. The huntsman took them back to the village and grandmother stayed with Little Red Riding Hood and her mother until she was well again. They all lived happily together and forgot all about the horrible Wolf.

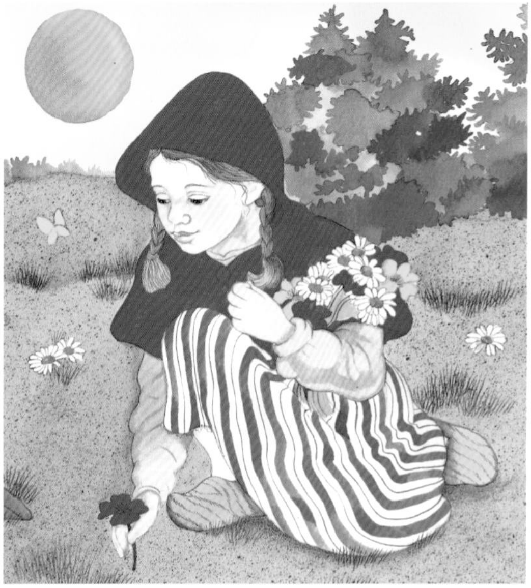

Series titles:

Snow White and the Seven Dwarfs
Cinderella
Puss in Boots
Sleeping Beauty
Beauty and the Beast
Little Red Riding Hood
Thumbelina
The Ugly Duckling
Hansel and Gretel
Town Mouse and Country Mouse
The Three Little Pigs
Pinocchio